Date: 11/18/22

**PALM BEACH COUNTY
LIBRARY SYSTEM**

**3650 Summit Boulevard
West Palm Beach, FL 33406**

DECONSTRUCTED DIETS

BLOW UP A BURGER

by Shalini Vallepur

BEARPORT PUBLISHING

Minneapolis, Minnesota

© 2021 Booklife Publishing

This edition is published by arrangement with Booklife Publishing.

North American adaptations © 2021 Bearport Publishing Company. All rights reserved. No part of this publication may be reproduced in whole or in part, stored in any retrieval system, or transmitted in any form or by any means, electronic, mechanical, photocopying, recording, or otherwise, without written permission from the publisher.

For more information, write to Bearport Publishing, 5357 Penn Avenue South, Minneapolis, MN 55419. Printed in the United States of America.

Library of Congress Cataloging-in-Publication Data is available at www.loc.gov or upon request from the publisher.

ISBN: 978-1-64747-521-5 (hardcover)
ISBN: 978-1-64747-528-4 (paperback)
ISBN: 978-1-64747-535-2 (ebook)

PHOTO CREDITS

All images are courtesy of Shutterstock.com, unless otherwise specified. With thanks to Getty Images, Thinkstock Photo, and iStockphoto. Front Cover - Big T, Tortuga, VWORLD. Recurring Images - Big T, VWORLD, Flas100, mything. 4-5 - mything, Nuk2013, Spotmatik Ltd. 6-7 - Alexander Prokopenko, LightField Studios, Tartila. 8-9 - AGorohov, Berns Images, Phill T. 10-11 - Abscent, Alfmaler, geniuscook_com, Tarasyuk Igor, WM. 12-13 - domnitsky, Pektoral, Ratana Prongjai, Tim UR, asantosg, Anna.zabella, mamormo. 14-15 - Breaking The Walls, Dima Sobko, LizavetaS, maglyvi, Sunnydream. 16-17 - Ekaterina Kondratova, Joshua Resnick, MSPhotographic, Zonda. 18-19 - xpixel, Amarante Ayo, Elegant Solution, neil langan OlgaChernyak, Reamolko, Elegant Solution. 20-21 - Brent Hofacker, ducu59us, fotoChef, Nina Firsova. 22-23 - Anna zabella, Brent Hofacker, brgfx, dikobraziy, Piotr Piatrouski

CONTENTS

What Is a Diet? **4**

Hungry for Hamburgers **6**

Blow Up a Burger **8**

Bun **10**

Veggies and Fruits **12**

Patty **14**

Cheese **16**

Sauces **18**

Smart Swaps **20**

Burgers around the World **22**

Glossary **24**

Index **24**

WHAT IS A DIET?

Your diet is what you eat and drink in a day. The foods we eat can help us grow and be healthy.

Most of the food we eat is made from many **ingredients**. Sometimes, it can be hard to know exactly what is in our food and where it comes from.

Cake can be made from milk, eggs, flour, and more.

Let's look at all the ingredients in a burger!

HUNGRY FOR HAMBURGERS

Burgers are often called hamburgers. This is because they are from the city of Hamburg in Germany.

Meat was made from Hamburg cows.

Cows

People from Hamburg moved to the United States. They started putting Hamburg meat between bread. This was a little like a burger.

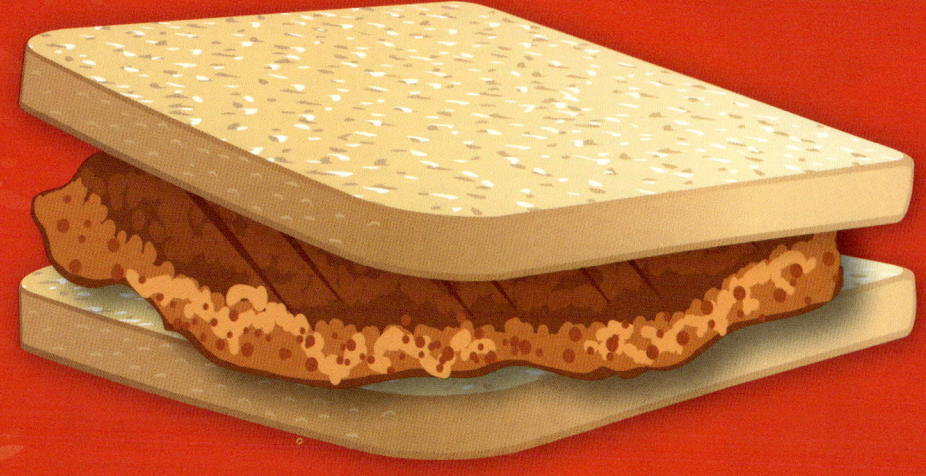

Over time, buns were used instead of slices of bread.

BLOW UP A BURGER

Burgers can have few or many ingredients.

Bun

Look at all those fruits and vegetables.

Tomato

Onion

Lettuce

Top a burger with whatever you like.

Pickle

Burger Patty

Cheese

Burger patties can be made of meat or vegetables.

DID YOU KNOW?
Around 50 billion burgers are eaten in the U.S. every year!

Let's learn about each ingredient.

9

BUN

A burger is held together by its bun. The bun is a type of bread that is made from **wheat**.

Wheat ......▶ White flour ......▶ Burger buns

Wheat is grown on farms. It is turned into flour. Flour is mixed with other ingredients to make buns.

Brioche bun

There are lots of different types of buns.

Sesame bun

Wheat can be made into different kinds of flour. Wheat flour is healthier for you than white flour.

Wheat ······▶ Wheat flour ······▶ Burger buns

Wheat buns have more **fiber** in them.

Seeded wheat bun

Wheat bun

VEGGIES AND FRUITS

Burgers can have lots of different toppings. Many people put vegetables and fruits on their burgers.

Lettuce → Chopped lettuce

Lettuce is usually chopped when put on a burger.

Tomato → Sliced tomato

Tomatoes can be sliced and put on burgers.

12

Onion — Sliced onion

Onions can give burgers crunch.

Pickle — Pickle slices

A cucumber is **pickled** to make pickles.

Veggies and fruits are tasty and healthy burger toppings.

PATTY

The main part of the burger is the patty. Patties can be made from animal meat.

Cow meat is called beef. Beef is ground up and made into patties.

Chicken meat is sometimes covered in breading when it is used in a burger.

Patties can be cooked in different ways.

Frying

You can fry patties in a hot pan.

Grilling

Many people grill patties over a fire.

CHEESE

Slices of cheese can be used as a burger topping. Cheese is made from milk.

Milk ••••▶ Cheddar cheese ••••▶ Cheddar cheese slices

Cheddar cheese is made from cow's milk.

American cheese has lots of extra ingredients added to it to make it last longer and look more yellow. It is less healthy for you.

American cheese slices

You can put cheese on your burger to make it a cheeseburger.

Burger

Cheeseburger

SAUCES

Many burgers are eaten with **sauces.**

Ketchup is made from tomatoes and lots of other ingredients.

Mustard seeds are mixed with different ingredients to make mustard.

Mayonnaise is a white sauce.

Some sauces have ingredients such as salt and sugar. Too much salt and sugar can be bad for our bodies.

Look for sauces that do not have added salt and sugar.

SMART SWAPS

Burgers are tasty, but too many of them can be unhealthy. Try swapping a meat patty for a vegetable patty.

Veggie burger

Vegetable patties are made from veggies instead of meat.

DIET SWAPS

Burgers can be made to fit lots of different diets by changing the ingredients.

A burger made with a veggie patty can be eaten in a **vegetarian** diet.

A burger with a bun that is not made of wheat can be eaten by people who can't have **gluten**.

Vegetarian burger

Gluten-free burger

BURGERS AROUND THE WORLD

People have come up with lots of yummy ways to enjoy burgers!

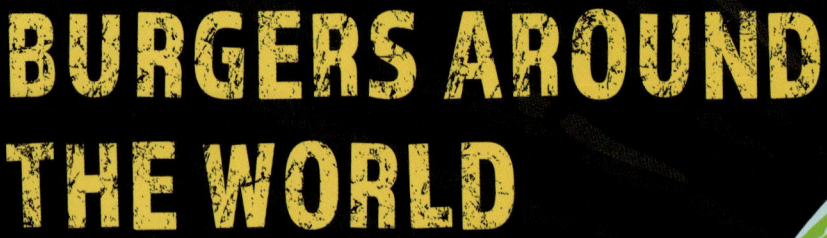

Ramen, a type of noodle from Japan, is used instead of a bun in this ramen burger.

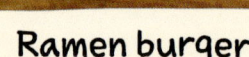

Ramen burger

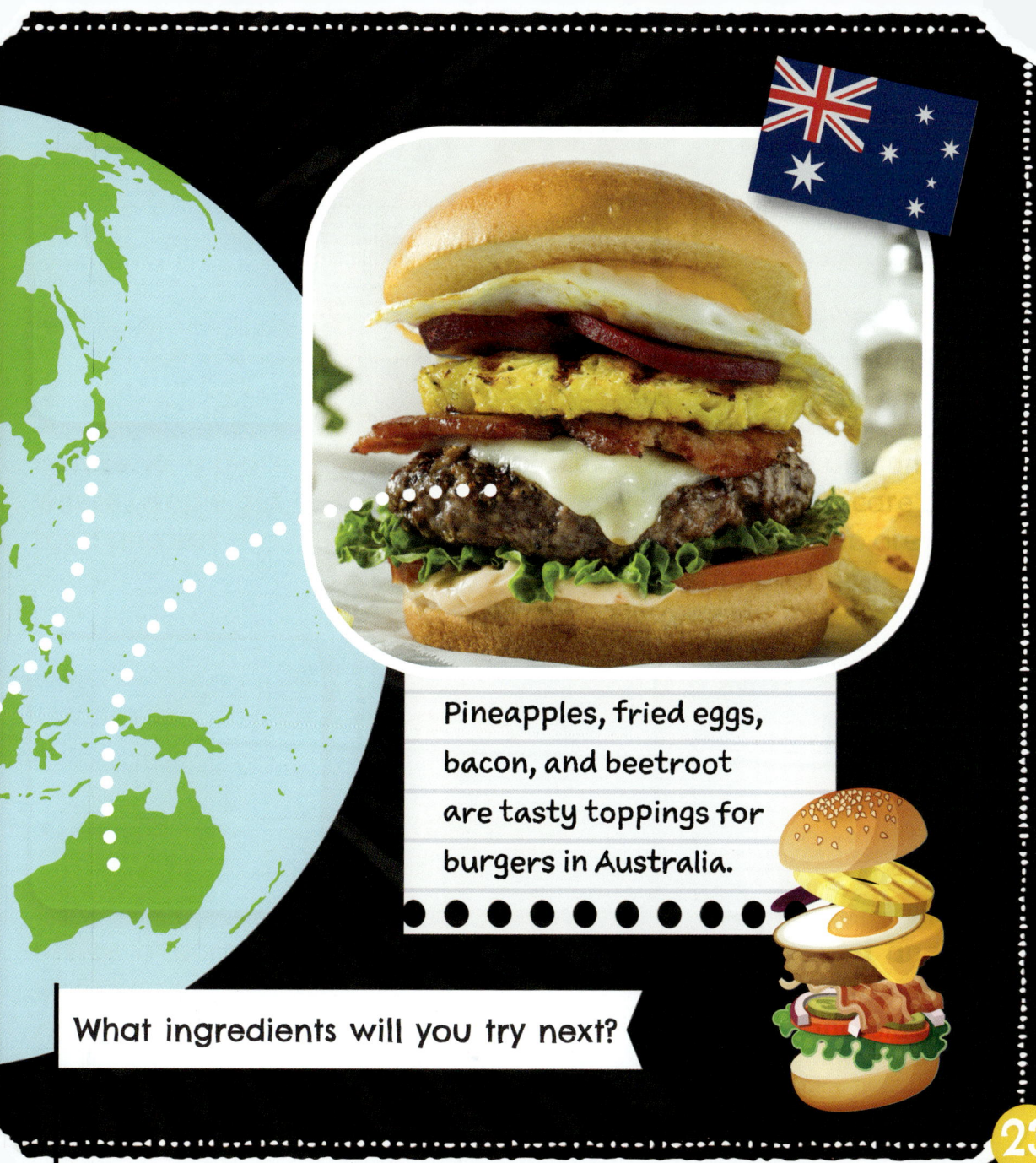

Pineapples, fried eggs, bacon, and beetroot are tasty toppings for burgers in Australia.

What ingredients will you try next?

GLOSSARY

fiber — a part of some foods that takes longer for the human body to break down

gluten — a part of wheat that makes bread dough sticky

ingredients — the different things that are used to make something

patty — a small, flat disk of chopped food

pickled — put in vinegar to make food last longer

sauces — liquid toppings for food

slices — thin pieces of food that are cut, or sliced, from something large

vegetarian — a diet where a person does not eat meat

wheat — a tall grass that is made into flour

INDEX

Australia 23
bread 7, 10, 14
chickens 14
cows 6, 14, 16
diets 4, 21
fruits 8, 12–13
Hamburg 6–7
Japan 22
patties 9, 14–15, 20–21
sauces 18–19
toppings 8, 12–13, 16, 23
vegetables 8–9, 12–13, 20–21